Jessica

"Get us a goal, Jess!" said Georgie.
Jessica aimed carefully, and the
ball went straight through the hoop.
  "Yesss!" cried Georgie, slapping
hands with Jessica.

*With grateful thanks to Kate Steel,
for all her help*

Make Friends With
Jessica

Ann Bryant

ORCHARD BOOKS

Chapter One

The new house was still quite a mess. There were boxes and pictures lying around everywhere. That was because Jessica and her family had only moved in a few days ago. The trouble with moving is that you don't know anyone at first. But luckily Jessica had met Chloe and they were already good friends.

Chloe had come home from school with Jessica and they'd been playing lots of games of hide-and-seek. It was great!

With all the boxes and clutter there were some really good hiding places. The trouble was, Jessica's two-year-old brother, Joseph wanted to play it over and over again.

"Play hi-seek?" he asked the girls for the tenth time.

Chloe and Jessica sighed.

"OK," said Jessica. "But it's the last game. Go and hide, Joseph."

The girls knew exactly where he was going to hide because he always hid in the same place.

"Bofe of you count vis time!" he said, sounding very excited.

The girls hid their faces with their hands so Joseph wouldn't be able to see that they were laughing. It didn't matter how they counted. Joseph couldn't tell if it was proper counting or not.

"One, two, skip a few, ninety-nine, a hundred!" the girls chanted together.

Chloe changed to a sing-song voice, "Coming...ready or not!"

Out of the corner of her eye she could see Joseph's little head poking out from behind one of the boxes. On his face was a huge grin. Jessica had to go right to the other end of the room, she was shaking with laughter so much. Chloe managed to keep a straight face as she pretended to search behind the other boxes, then the curtain, the settee and both chairs. And finally she made out that she'd only just spotted him.

"There you are! What a good hiding place, Joseph."

Jessica turned round and clapped her hands together. "Brilliant, Joseph!"

Joseph laughed his socks off. "'Nother game?" he said, jumping up and down wildly.

But their mum came in from the kitchen at that moment, with Chloe's mum just behind her.

"It's not time to go already, is it?" Chloe asked.

"'Fraid so," said her mum. "But Jessica can come for tea one day next week."

When they'd gone Jessica's mum frowned at all the mess. "The trouble with moving into a new house is that it takes so long to unpack," she said.

"Can I help?" said Jessica. She was thinking that anything would be better than yet another game of hide-and-seek with Joseph.

"You can help me later if you want,

but right now I've got a treat for you," smiled Jessica's mum.

A lovely warm feeling spread all over Jessica. She loved treats.

"What?" she asked excitedly.

"You're going to have a swimming lesson!" said her mum.

The warm feeling seeped away in a flash. "I don't want a swimming lesson," growled Jessica. "That's not a treat! That's yuk!"

"Don't be silly…"

"I'm not being silly. I hate swimming lessons."

"But why? You were getting on so well in your old lessons? It'll be great! You'll see. Run upstairs and find your costume, there's a good girl."

Jessica ran upstairs, but she didn't find her costume. Instead she curled up into

a tight little ball with her duvet wrapped round her. She knew she was acting like a baby but she couldn't help it.

Chapter Two

"I'm not going swimming," Jessica mumbled to herself. "I'll be the only one with armbands on."

Jessica lay on the bed, remembering the swimming lessons she'd had before they'd moved house. There had been ten children in the class. All the others had taken their armbands off by the third lesson. But Jessica hadn't quite dared. She'd told her mum she thought she might take them off in the next lesson though. But that's when she stopped having swimming lessons because her family moved here, to the town where Jessica's granny lived.

That last swimming lesson seemed ages ago. Jessica started thinking scary thoughts about what might happen in her new lessons.

What if the new teacher is horrible and strict? What if she thinks I'm silly for not daring to take my armbands off? What if she *makes* me take them off and I go under and swallow lots of water and can't breathe and no one notices?

No, there was definitely no way Jessica was going to go swimming now. It would have been better if Chloe had been in the same class. But Chloe went on Tuesdays.

That gave Jessica an idea. She raced

downstairs and said to her mum, "Why can't I go on Tuesdays with Chloe?"

"Because the Tuesday sessions are all for children who can swim already. I've booked you in with the children with armbands. So you've got nothing to worry about."

"That means I'll be with the little ones!" shouted Jessica.

"I expect they'll be all sorts of ages," said her mum. "Come on, love. We don't want to be late the first time you go. Have you found your costume?"

And that gave Jessica another idea. "No, I've looked everywhere but it seems to be missing."

"Let *me* look," said her mother, pursing her lips and going towards the stairs.

Uh-oh! Her mum would find it straight away. Jessica had to think of a way of getting up to her bedroom before her mum did so she could hide the costume. There was no time to lose. Her eyes darted round the living room. Perfect! Her little brother was trying to climb inside one of the boxes.

"Joseph's going to break those special plates in there," she said, sounding very alarmed. Then she raced upstairs, while her mum went to get Joseph out of the box.

In her room, Jessica knew exactly which drawer to open. She yanked out her swimsuit but it seemed to be stuck. "Come on, you stupid thing," she said, tugging harder because she could hear her mum's footsteps on the stairs. Then out came the swimsuit and *in* came her mum.

"You found it! Well done," said her

mum, smiling. "Wrap it up in this towel and put it in your bag. Then come straight downstairs. I'll be getting Joseph in the car."

The moment her mother had gone out, Jessica heaved a huge sigh.

"I wish swimming had never been invented!" she said, chucking her costume on the bed.

Chapter Three

The leisure centre stank of chlorine. It reminded Jessica of her swimming lessons where she used to live. She begged to go back home the moment they got through the door.

"I'll learn to swim when I'm older," she said in a pleading voice, as she and her mum went up to the main desk.

"No, it's best to learn when you're young."

Jessica walked to the changing room

in her very slowest walk, hoping she might be too late. Then they could go home. Joseph seemed to think it was quite funny to push her bottom from behind. And that made Jessica mad.

"Get off, Joseph!" she said angrily.

"Joseph, leave Jessie alone," said her mum.

Joseph did as he was told.

"You don't have to come in the cubicle with me," said Jessica, thinking she could waste a bit more time by getting changed extra slowly. "I can manage on my own."

Her mum was pleased that Jessica was being so grown-up. "I'll wait just outside then. Be quick."

Twice her mum called through the door for Jessica to hurry up, and even Joseph shouted, "Hurrup, Jessie!"

Then when at last she was ready her mum put her clothes in a locker and gave Jessica the key on an elastic band.

"Go and stand on the side with the others," she whispered. "Look, there's the teacher."

"Where?"

Jessica couldn't see any sign of a teacher. She looked out towards the pool. And as she turned she caught sight of her back view in a mirror. She gasped. There, right in the middle of her costume, across her bottom, was a hole. It hadn't been there the last time Jessica had gone swimming before they moved. So how on earth...?

Jessica suddenly remembered what had happened in her room. When she'd pulled the costume out of the drawer it had got stuck at first and she'd tugged even harder. It must have been caught on a sharp little piece of wood or something, and because she'd yanked so hard, it had torn.

Her mum was waving at a man. Jessica just stood there, rooted to the spot.

"Hello Jessica. My name's Mark," he called. "Good news! The water's very warm today."

Jessica put her hands behind her to cover the hole. She wanted to tell her mum she couldn't have a swimming lesson now because of the hole. But Mark was smiling and beckoning. Her mum gave Jessica a little push and she set off towards the pool. She kept her hands behind her though.

"Joseph swim?" her little brother said. Her mum ignored him. She was watching Jessica and wondering why she was walking in that funny way with her hands on her bottom.

Joseph didn't like being ignored. "Joseph swim!" he shouted. His voice echoed all round the pool. He smiled at the sound of it, and started shouting loudly over and over again, "Joseph swim!"

"Shush!" said his mum. But he took no notice. "Jess!" she called, "I'll take him for a walk, love. See you soon."

Jessica just nodded.

There were five girls and two boys waiting by the side of the pool. They were all wearing armbands, but they all looked much younger than Jessica. She felt tall and silly standing beside them.

"This is Jessica," said Mark to the others.

All the children stared at her.

"How old are you?" asked one of the boys.

"Eight," said Jessica.

"Can't you even swim yet?" the boy went on.

Jessica went red. She didn't say anything because she couldn't think of a good answer.

"OK, one at a time down the steps," said Mark. "Remember, no running."

One by one they all plopped in and started splashing about. Then even Mark got in, so there was only Jessica left on the side. She didn't know what to do. It was impossible to get down the steps without holding on to the rails. And if she did that everyone would see her bottom.

"It doesn't matter if you don't want

to get in just yet," Mark said in a kind voice. "Tell you what, you can be my helper. See those floats over there? Can you throw them in one at a time?"

Jessica would have loved that job but there was still the problem of not being able to move her hands away from her bottom. If the other children saw her torn swimsuit she'd feel terrible. They'd probably laugh and point and say nasty things.

She didn't know what to do, so she just stood there wishing that her mum had stayed. Then she could plead with her to be allowed to go home. Just when Jessica thought she was going to cry she noticed that none of the children were looking and neither was Mark. Quick as a flash she sat down and plopped into the pool from the side.

What a relief! The hole was safely hidden under water now.

Chapter Four

Mark smiled to see her in the pool.

"Right everybody, let's have a running race," he called out. "All line up at the side."

Jessica stood on the end of the line in the deepest water.

"On your marks, get set, go!" called Mark.

Jessica had done this before at her old lessons so she didn't have anything to worry about. In fact she was feeling better every second. She kicked the water as she ran across, striding out as hard as she could. There was so much water being splashed about everywhere that she didn't know who reached the other side first until Mark called out, "Brilliant, Jessica! You won!"

The boy next to her was really scowling. "That's because she's the biggest," he said to Mark. "It's not fair."

Mark just ignored him. "Let's try some jumping," he said. "See who can jump the highest."

Jessica only did little jumps so Mark wouldn't tell her she was the best. She didn't want that boy to be cross again.

"Come on, Jessica," said Mark. "You can go higher than that. Bend those knees and give a big push."

Jessica wanted to please Mark. He was

so nice and kind. It had been great
when he'd told her she was brilliant.
She did as he'd said, bending her knees
as far as she could without her face
going under. Then she pushed with her
feet and bounced up. It was a wonderful
feeling. She did it again and again.

"Very good, Christopher!" called Mark.

"Am I going higher than that new
girl?" Christopher called back.

Jessica saw that Christopher was the
boy who had said it wasn't fair when
she'd won the race.

"Not quite," Mark shouted above the
splashing noises.

Jessica decided not to try so hard so
Christopher could go higher. She did
one last big bounce. And that's when
She heard his loud voice ringing round
the pool.

"That girl's got a hole in her swimsuit! I can see her bum!"

He giggled loudly and then everyone was giggling.

Jessica felt as though someone had kicked her in the tummy. She'd completely forgotten about the hole. She stopped jumping and stood perfectly still like a ball that had lost its bounce. All around her, the other children laughed and pointed as they jumped and splashed. She put her hands over her ears to cut out the awful noise. Then she tried to run to the steps. Everyone was staring at her and her legs were all shaky, not strong like they had been in the race.

As she climbed the steps the laughter grew louder and louder. No one could tell she was crying because of all the water on her face. The moment she was out of the pool she ran towards the changing rooms.

"Don't run. It's slippery!" called out Mark.

But he was too late. Jessica had fallen on her bottom. And it was agony. Now she didn't know whether she was crying about the hole or the fall. All she knew was that her mum was bending down with her arm round her, saying, "It's all right, love. I'm here now."

Chapter Five

It was Sunday morning and Jessica was in the leisure centre pool with her mum, her dad, Joseph and Chloe. She was wearing her brand new black and white swimming costume. It was absolutely wicked.

"Help!" cried Jessica's dad, as Jessica and Chloe climbed on his back. "I'm being attacked by a couple of monsters!"

Jessica's mum just laughed.

"I thought you said you wore armbands," said Chloe to Jessica.

"I do for swimming," Jessica explained.

"But you *are* swimming," said Chloe.

"This isn't swimming — it's only playing," said Jessica.

"No, Chloe's right," said Jessica's dad. "This is really no different from swimming. I bet you could swim right across the pool with no armbands if you tried."

"Yes, go on, Jess," said Chloe, nodding and smiling.

Jessica took a deep breath and set off from the side. Her dad walked backwards just in front of her, his hands stretched out in case Jessica needed to grab hold of them. But she managed completely on her own.

"I did it! I did it!" she cried, jumping up and down at the other side of the pool. "I can go to a different swimming lesson now – and no armbands! Yesss!"

So now it was the next Wednesday and
Jessica was on her way to the leisure
centre. Only she was going to a later
class. A class with older children.

She didn't mind the chlorine smell at
all as she went in at the main entrance.
It was going to be great with a brand
new costume and no armbands. Nobody
would laugh at her today. These were
different children who didn't know
anything about her holey costume.

In the changing room Jessica felt a bit
nervous though. What if Mark said
something about the hole?

"I don't want Mark to tell anyone
about...my other swimsuit," she said
to her mum as she put her clothes in
the locker.

"He wouldn't dream of saying anything," her mum assured her. "I'm taking Joseph to the swings. I'll be back at the end to collect you. OK?"

So Jessica went to line up on the side with the others. There were only two boys and three girls.

"Just three more to come," said Mark. "Then we'll get started."

Jessica was glad she wasn't the last one to arrive. This swimming lesson was going to be a million times better than the last one. She could tell.

When everyone was there, Mark told them all to sit down on the edge and slide in. After some hard kicks and high jumps they did a Superman race with the floats, then Mark said they were going to practise the leg action for front crawl.

"Hold on to the side with two hands," he called.

But they'd no sooner lined up than another voice rang round the pool for everyone to hear. Jessica recognised the voice. It was Christopher's.

"Kayley! Look! There's that girl with a hole in her bum!" he shrieked.

Jessica went stiff. She jerked her head round to see Christopher with wet hair, leaning over the bit where you watch. He was shouting to the girl next to her and she was staring at Jessica with a big grin on her face. She must be Christopher's sister. She looked just like him.

"Quiet please," said Mark. "Let's get on."

But Kayley was whispering to the girl next to her and they both moved away from Jessica. Then Kayley flapped her hand at the girl on the other side of Jessica. She was telling her to move away too.

Jessica was left in a big space on her own. She felt even worse than she had done in the last lesson. If only she hadn't wanted to hide her stupid swimsuit, none of this would be happening.

"That's right, feet like flippers. Keep your legs close together," Mark was saying. But all Jessica could hear was... *that girl with a hole in her bum.*

She thought about getting out of the pool and running back to the changing rooms. But then she remembered what had happened last time. So she just stood there with a big lump in her throat.

"OK, everyone, find a partner," said Mark.

Kayley grabbed another girl's hand.

"Phew, I thought I was going to get landed with Holey Bum just then!" she said, rolling her eyes.

Mark didn't hear. "I'll be your partner, Jessica," he said. "But don't worry, we're one short this week. Next week you'll have a proper partner."

Whenever Kayley wasn't looking, Jessica sneaked looks at her. She was sure she recognised her from school, but it was hard to recognise people when their hair was all wet.

There were lots of other things to practise in pairs, and Jessica was always with Mark. Kayley pulled faces at Jessica whenever Mark wasn't looking. But she couldn't call out any more nasty names because Mark would have heard.

At the end of the session, Jessica walked to the changing rooms on her own. And that's when the worst thing of all happened. From behind her she could hear Kayley and her friends chanting, "Holey Bum, Holey Bum, we hate Holey Bum," over and over again.

Jessica decided something at that moment. She was never coming back here again. Even if her mum stopped her pocket money for a whole year and threw away the television. She was still never coming back to the horrible stinky leisure centre.

Chapter Six

It was playtime at school the next day. Jessica was waiting by the climbing frame for Chloe to come back from the loo. She was watching the cloakroom door. Chloe would be coming out any second. But Jessica got a shock because the next time the door opened it wasn't Chloe. It was Kayley. Jessica quickly turned away but she was too late. Kayley had spotted her.

"That's the girl I told you about,"

came the hateful voice. "You know –
the one with the holey swimsuit." Jessica
pretended she hadn't heard. She started
climbing up the climbing frame.

"Hey, Molly, I wonder if she wears
holey knickers too," Kayley went on.

The lump came back in Jessica's
throat. She quickly got down from the
climbing frame. She could see Kayley
whispering to two girls called Bethany
and Anna. Then they all pointed at
her and laughed. Jessica didn't know
what to do, so she pretended she could
see Chloe coming back.

"Hi Chloe!" she called, as she ran off.

"Talking to herself now!" screeched
Kayley. And the girls around her
burst out laughing.

Chloe really did come back just
after that.

"Just ignore them. They're nasty!" she said fiercely when Jessica told her what had happened.

It was all right all the time Chloe was playing with her, but Jessica was dreading being on her own, in case Kayley was mean to her.

When the whistle for the end of playtime went, everyone lined up in classes. The teacher on duty asked Chloe to go and tell the other teachers that the children were coming in.

Kayley and her friends were in the line next to Jessica's. The teacher's back was turned, and Jessica saw Kayley whisper to Molly. Then they both looked at Jessica and giggled. Jessica stared straight ahead of her, pretending not to notice, but a scary shiver was creeping all over her body. Kayley was sneaking into

Jessica's line, right behind Jessica. Jessica's line went quiet. No one would dare tell on Kayley Carr.

Still Jessica stared straight ahead of her, but she could feel her face going red. She was praying that Chloe would come back and rescue her, but God must have been busy because he didn't answer.

Something was wrong but Jessica couldn't work out what. It was as though a big breeze was rushing round the tops of her legs, making her suddenly cold. And just at that very moment the teacher's furious voice made everyone stand still as statues.

"Kayley Carr! What DO you think you're doing! Go inside this minute! Wait outside my classroom and I'll deal with you when I come in."

Jessica felt something move behind her.

It was her skirt falling into place. She realised that Kayley must have pulled it up at the back. It made her cheeks go hot just thinking about it. Fancy not even noticing what Kayley was doing. She could have kicked herself. The teacher had noticed though. And now Kayley was in for a big telling-off.

"I'll get you for this," she hissed in Jessica's ear as she stomped off.

Jessica just carried on staring straight ahead of her, but inside her heart was beating loudly.

Chapter Seven

At school the next day Jessica and Chloe were playing on the other side of the playground from Kayley Carr and her friends.

"They're not really her friends," Chloe told Jessica. "They're just scared of her, so they do what she says and they laugh at her jokes. We don't care about them. We've got plenty of friends of our own."

And it was true. It was such a big school that lots of children didn't know

  42

anything about Jessica and the holey swimsuit.

"But what if Kayley gets a gang against us?" said Jessica.

"She won't," said Chloe simply.

But Jessica wasn't so sure. She hated the thought of gangs. But more than that she hated the thought of the next swimming lesson.

"I'm not going to swimming lessons any more," Jessica told Chloe.

"Does your mum mind?" asked Chloe.

"I haven't told her yet. But I'm definitely not," said Jessica.

That afternoon it was Outside PE.

"We're joining up with Mrs Ballam's class," said Jessica's teacher, Miss Dixon. "We'll have a game of basketball."

A big cheer went up. Everyone liked

basket ball. Jessica liked it too, but she wasn't cheering with the others. She knew who was in Mrs Ballam's class. Kayley Carr.

"I'll choose the teams from the register," said Miss Dixon. "There are a lot of you, so I want everyone on their best behaviour. I'm calling the two teams the Yellows and the Reds."

Jessica prayed that she'd be on the same team as Kayley. Then at least Kayley might not be so horrid.

This time the prayer was answered. Jessica and Kayley were both on the Yellows. The only sad thing was that Chloe was on the Reds.

Kayley came and stood beside Jessica, and Jessica thought for a minute that she might be going to be nice to her. But Kayley just said, "Hello, your

Royal *Holey*-ness out of the corner of her mouth, then ran back giggling to the others.

Jessica looked at the ground.

"She's stupid!" said Chloe.

"Now remember, you can run while you're holding the ball," said Miss Dixon. "But only run a few steps before you pass it to someone else. If anyone runs for too long I'll blow my whistle and the other team will be allowed to have the ball. Is everybody clear?"

Jessica glanced at Kayley. She was whispering to a group of girls who were all on her team.

"I bet she's whispering about me," said Jessica.

"It's all right, she can't do anything with Miss Dixon there," Chloe said quietly.

When the game started Kayley didn't pay any attention at all to Jessica. Jessica stopped worrying quite so much. Maybe Kayley had been whispering to her friends about something that was nothing to do with her.

The other team made a good start. They scored two goals almost straight away. Jessica wished *her* team would get the ball then they'd stand a chance of scoring a goal.

Just as she was thinking this, Bethany, from the Yellows, managed to get the ball.

"Well done, Bethany," said Kayley.

Bethany passed the ball to Rachel, Rachel passed it to Tom and Tom scored a goal.

"Two to the Reds, one to the Yellows," said Miss Dixon. Then she blew her whistle for the game to carry on.

This time Kayley got hold of the ball first. She passed it to Anna. Anna looked round. She saw Jessica standing quite near the hoop. "Here, Anna," said Jessica, holding her hands out. But Anna threw it to Rachel instead. Rachel couldn't catch it and the other team got it.

They didn't score a goal though because Alex from the Yellows managed to get it back. He threw it to Molly.

"Here Molly," said Jessica, holding out her hands, because she was really near the hoop now and she knew she could get the ball through it and score a goal, if only Molly would pass it to her.

Molly definitely saw Jessica. But she deliberately turned the other way and threw the ball to Ollie. Ollie dropped it because he was too far away.

"You should have thrown it to Jessica, Molly," said Miss Dixon.

Molly didn't say anything, but she gave Kayley a sly look. Jessica saw the look and her legs went all shaky.

She suddenly realised what Kayley's whispering had been all about. Kayley must have told all the girls on her team not to pass the ball to Jessica. They were acting as though she wasn't even on their team.

She might as well have been invisible.

Chapter Eight

The game carried on. Miss Dixon didn't realise what Kayley and the others were doing. Even Chloe didn't realise. But Jessica knew, and Kayley knew she knew.

There was no point in Jessica holding out her hands and saying, "Here, pass it to me!" because everyone just ignored her. At least, the girls did. Kayley hadn't whispered to any boys, so Jessica's only chance of getting the ball was if a boy passed it to her. The trouble was, the boys usually passed it to other boys. So Jessica had to pretend she didn't care. She ran about with the others, and cheered when her team got a goal. But she hardly ever touched the ball.

The game seemed to go on and on. Jessica was sure that Outside PE didn't usually last as long as this. She supposed it was because time seems to pass more quickly when you're having fun. And right now, Jessica was definitely not having fun. She just wanted the game to be over, and the home-time bell to ring.

The Yellows had the ball.

"Here, Kayley," said Alex.

Kayley passed him the ball and he threw it to Jessica. Jessica felt as though a little ray of sunshine had popped out for two seconds in a cloudy grey sky. The nearest person she could pass the ball to now, was Kayley. She threw it carefully and Kayley caught it. But then she dropped it on purpose.

"Butterfingers, Kayley!" said Miss Dixon. "Go on, Chloe! Pick it up!"

Kayley waited till Miss Dixon wasn't watching, then she looked at her hands. As she looked, she pulled a big face as though there was something disgusting on her hands that had been on the ball. Jessica knew exactly what Kayley was doing. She was pretending she'd caught a horrible disease off Jessica. As Kayley wiped her hands on her PE shorts, all her friends laughed.

Chloe didn't notice because she was right in the middle of scoring a goal for the Reds.

"That's five to the Reds and five to the Yellows!" said Miss Dixon. "Whichever team gets the next goal wins."

Alex, from the Yellows, got the ball and passed it to Ollie. Ollie passed it to Georgie and Georgie passed it to Jessica!

Jessica nearly dropped it, she was so surprised. Georgie was one of the girls who had been in the whispering group with Kayley before the game started.

All the other girls from the Yellows were looking anxiously at Kayley, wondering what she was going to do. It looked like Georgie was in big trouble. But she didn't seem at all bothered.

"Get us a goal, Jess. Go on!" she said.

Jessica aimed carefully and the ball went straight through the middle of the hoop.

"Yesss!" cried Georgie, slapping hands with Jessica.

"Well done, Jessica," said Miss Dixon. "Game over. The Yellows have won,

6–5. We're a bit late so run back quickly and get changed."

Everybody started charging back to the cloakroom.

"That was wicked!" said Chloe to Jessica. Jessica was still feeling shocked that Georgie had dared to pass her the ball. She looked behind to see if Kayley was being horrible to Georgie.

But she wasn't. Quite the opposite in fact. Kayley and Rachel were giving Georgie a King's Carry, and Georgie was punching her fist in the air saying a rap. She looked like a proper rapper. Her whole body seemed to be dancing even though she was sitting down.

"Big goal!
Big dream!
Big respect for the yellow team!"

"Let's have a bit of hush!" said Miss Dixon.

Then Georgie suddenly jumped off the chair and came running up to Chloe and Jessica.

"Give us a King's Carry!" she said.

Chloe and Jessica linked hands and Georgie jumped on. Then she said the rap again as they walked along.

"Big goal!
Big dream!
Big respect for the yellow team!"

Jessica wished *she* could be like Georgie. Georgie didn't care what anyone thought. She just did what she wanted.

❀ ❀ ❀

Chapter Nine

Jessica was sitting on the top stair. Her mum was standing at the bottom of the stairs.

"I've told you, I *hate* swimming. I don't want to go. I can swim already. Why do I need lessons?"

"Because you need to learn the proper strokes. At the moment you can only do doggy-paddle."

"It's cruel making me go when I hate it."

"I don't you think you *do* hate it. I think someone is being nasty to you, and *that's* what you hate."

Jessica opened her mouth to speak but then she shut it again. Her mum was right. However had she guessed?

"I'm still not going," mumbled Jessica.

"I'll have a word with Mark and everything will be fine."

"No it won't. You don't know what Kayley can be like."

Jessica bit her lip. She'd said Kayley's name by mistake.

"Don't worry, I won't mention any names," said Jessica's mum. "I'll stay and watch. No one will be nasty if I'm watching. Now go and get your things. No argument!"

All the way to the leisure centre Jessica thought about Georgie. *She* wouldn't care less that Kayley was going to be there. If only Jessica could be like Georgie. Maybe she should try. All you have to do is pretend you don't care about anything. Easy!

I don't care about the smell, said Jessica to herself as she went inside the leisure centre.

I don't care about the wet floor, she told herself in the changing room.

I don't care that Kayley is there, she kept repeating, as she walked towards the pool.

"Oh good, you're here, Jessica," said Mark. "That just leaves two people to come. We'll just wait one more minute."

"Billy's ill," said one of the girls.

"Oh right, so we're just waiting for the girl who was away last week...

What's her name?"

"Georgie," Kayley told him. "She's in my class at school. She's definitely coming."

Jessica gasped. Georgie was going to be in the swimming lesson! Brilliant! And just then Georgie appeared.

"Georgie!" Kayley called out. "Stand here. Next to me."

"No, I'll go here," said Georgie. And she squeezed into the space between Jessica and the girl next to her. Jessica couldn't believe it. Her whole body felt as though it was dancing. Just like Georgie's had done on the King's Carry.

"Right, everyone sit down and slide yourselves into the pool carefully," said Mark.

Jessica did it straight away. So did everyone else. Well, nearly everyone else.

Georgie sat down but she didn't get in the pool. She just squirmed her bottom about.

"You can go down the steps if you want, Georgie," said Mark.

And Jessica watched in amazement as Georgie went slowly down the steps then clung hard to the side of the pool.

"Scaredy cat!" called Kayley from the other side.

"Big boss face!" Jessica called back to Kayley, before she'd had time to even think what she was saying.

Kayley looked as surprised as if a big fish had bitten her bottom.

Jessica giggled as she swam over to Georgie.

I've done it! I've actually stood up to her! she said to herself, feeling like the happiest girl in the world.

"OK, warm up with great big jumps," said Mark. "Hold on to the side if you want."

Jessica knew that Mark was watching Georgie and feeling sorry for her. It's impossible to jump properly when you're holding on to the side.

"Try those big jumps with a partner now," said Mark.

"I'll be yours, Georgie," yelled Kayley across the pool.

"Actually I'd rather be with *you*, Jess?" Georgie whispered.

Jessica didn't say anything but inside her body she was shouting *yes!*

So they started jumping together, and Kayley glared at them from across the pool. Jessica made sure she only did little jumps so Georgie's face wouldn't go under much.

"Well done, you two," said Mark. "I'll be your partner, Kayley. Don't look so cross!"

Kayley's face was one big scowl. Christopher, Kayley's brother, pointed at her from the watching area.

"Look at Kayley. Doesn't she look stupid jumping with the teacher!" he laughed.

Jessica caught her mum's eye. She was sitting right next to Christopher. She gave Jessica a thumbs-up signal. But Jessica couldn't give one back because Georgie was gripping her hands so tightly.

As soon as Jessica felt Georgie's grip go a bit slacker, she jumped a bit higher and Georgie did too. She didn't seem to mind so much about getting her face wet any more.

"This is good," said Georgie. "I'm

not scared any more."

"Neither am I!" said Jessica. And she really meant it.

Then together they jumped higher and higher... And even higher!

Look out for...

Make Friends With

Georgie

Someone's spotted **Georgie**'s talents –
she's going to be a star!

Make Friends With

(1) **Chloe ★ Jessica**   1 84121 734 4   £3.99 ☐

(2) **Georgie ★ Megan**   1 84121 784 0   £3.99 ☐

(3) **Lily ★ Izzie**   1 84121 786 7   £3.99 ☐

(4) **Claire ★ Lauren**   1 84121 790 5   £3.99 ☐

(5) **Yasmin ★ Lucy**   1 84121 792 1   £3.99 ☐

(6) **Rachel ★ Zoe**   1 84121 794 8   £3.99 ☐

(7) **Jade ★ Amy**   1 84121 796 4   £3.99 ☐

(8) **Hannah ★ Poppy**   1 84121 798 0   £3.99 ☐

Who will YOU meet next?

Make Friends With books are available from all good bookshops,
or can be ordered direct from the publisher:
Orchard Books, PO BOX 29, Douglas IM99 1BQ
Credit card orders please telephone 01624 836000
or fax 01624 837033
or e-mail: bookshop@enterprise.net for details.

To order please quote title, author and ISBN
and your full name and address.
Cheques and postal orders should be made payable to
'Bookpost plc.'
Postage and packing is FREE within the UK
(overseas customers should add £1.00 per book).

Prices and availability are subject to change.

Coming up next in...

Make Friends With Jessica

Who'll save the day for Jessica when she finds herself in too deep?

Flip me over!